Dorian Haarhoff

Desert December

Illustrated by Leon Vermeulen

Young Piper
PAN MACMILLAN
CHILDREN'S BOOKS

Seth lived in the Kuiseb Canyon, not far from the sea, in a small house with his mother and his grandfather. His father was mostly away, working inland on a copper mine.

Fresh water flowed where this small community had its home and where the zebra came to drink. Sometimes the fog blew in, with its clammy breath. Sometimes the sun sucked the water pools like a hungry baby at the breast.

Then Seth had to dig holes and draw water up in tins. Grandfather Nampa helped him carry the tins on a long stick. They made up songs as they walked, for Seth loved to sing.

Seth had been in the Canyon for as long as he could remember. He went to school in a house made of stone. His grandfather had been one of the builders. His long hands with lizard fingers had flicked away in the hot sun.

One day, early in December, Seth's mother called him to her.

'I am going to the village at the mine,' she told him.

'Will you be gone a long time?' the boy asked.

'I shall stay there until our baby is born,' she answered. 'Grandfather Nampa will look after you.'

'Can't you have the baby here?'

'No, Seth. There is a midwife at the village and I want to be near your father.'

Then she left. Seth missed her especially when the sun set.

'Why don't you make her something?'
suggested his grandfather. So the old
man taught him to carve shapes out of
bits of wood brought down by the river.

Seth carved her a figure. When he had finished he told his Grandfather Nampa that he wanted to take it to her. Grandfather thought for a while, his fingers pulling at his left ear. He thought better that way. Then he said, 'That's a good idea. You go to your mother.'

So one Namib evening, just one day before Christmas, Seth whistled their donkeys to him. He hitched them to the cart. Seth was proud of that cart. He had helped his father build it before he left for the copper mine. As he ran his hand against the side of the donkey-cart, he remembered how they had brought a packing case from the harbour. The wheels they had taken off an old car, rusted the colour of the desert. The shaft had been cut out of an old doorpost.

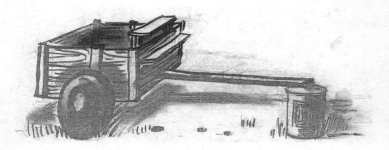

Seth packed the cart. He wrapped his mother's gift in an old *Namib News* that had blown across the dunes. He carefully placed it in the cart among the cheese and bread, the donkey fodder and a goatskin water-bag. Seth made a cushion from his rolled-up blanket bought at the all-sorts store.

The sun was floating on the sea by the time he had harnessed the donkeys. His grandfather came outside to see him off.

'How shall I find the village?' he asked him. The old man tugged his ear. 'You will get there. My old bones tell me that.'

Then he pointed into the desert. 'That is the way you must go. Inland, with the sea behind your back. You'll know your father's shack because there's an old rusted drum next to it – high as a sand-dune.'

'Goodbye, Grandpa!'

'Goodbye, Seth. Go well, my boy.'

The earth tilted to soft half-darkness as
Seth travelled. Away from the sea he was
going, in the direction of the rising sun.
The cart rolled along in the twilight of a
December night.

Above him, the Namib stars were
dimmed by a white moon.

Seth's journey would take a whole night and a whole day, across ground he'd never seen before. But as he went along he too began to feel that he would find the place – 'My young bones tell me that!'

Much later, an old man suddenly appeared on the side of the dust road. He was wearing an old mealie sack around his shoulders to keep out the cold of the desert night.

'Hullo, Oupa,' called Seth.

'Hullo boy,' said the old man and he smiled at Seth. His teeth were the colour of the little golden mole that rolls down the dunes.

'I'm going to that farmhouse,' he pointed. 'Take me with you.'

He climbed up and they rode off along a bumpy track. After a while the old man broke off a piece of Nara plant that he was chewing. He had rolled out the desert squash and dried the pips and sap in the sun. 'Here you are,' he said. 'Have a piece of *veldkos*. You look as if you're going on an important journey and this will give you strength.' Seth chewed a piece of its pumpkin-coloured sweetness, leaving a little Nara next to his mother's present.

The old man did not speak again. When they reached the farmhouse he got off and waved goodbye. He reminded Seth of his own grandfather – quiet, like the desert.

To keep the loneliness out of his ears Seth thought of the song of the cicadas, the beetles in the thorn-tree thickets. The thorns were as white as the Christmas pictures in an old missionary's book. The song was sun yellow.

The cicadas sing in sunlight
When the day is newly born.
The song runs along the leaf
To the edge of a long white thorn.

Seth thought of all the small desert
creatures he knew. His favourite was the
black Onymacris beetle which collects
fog on its back. In the warming sun, the
fog trickles down its shell into a waiting
mouth. 'I want to be clever like that,'
thought Seth.

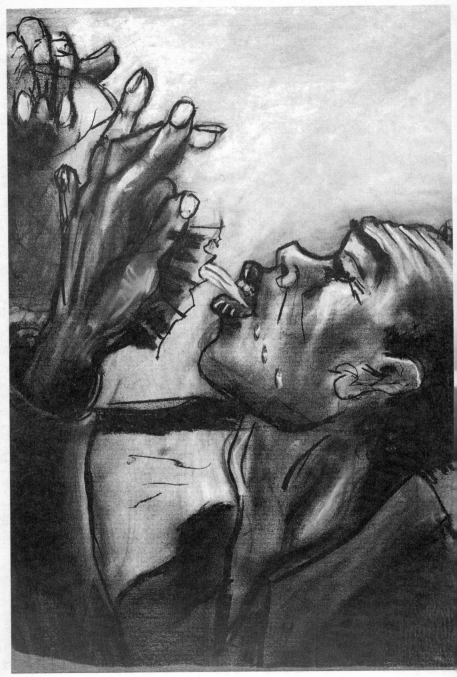

While the moon was swollen like a giant desert melon, Seth met a thirsty miner who was returning from the mine.

He wore old shoes that let in the desert. After they had greeted each other, the miner spoke. 'I want a drink of water.' Seth gave him the dripping goatskin bag and the young man drank long and deep.

Then he took out of his pocket a small rock and pressed it into Seth's hand. Seth turned the honey-coloured rock between his fingers.

'Look closely and you will see copper stars,' said the miner. When Seth looked up again the young man had continued on his way.

Seth travelled towards the new day. The moon and the sun seemed to be balanced on a giant see-saw. Then the weight of the moon going down seemed to lift the sun into the sky.

Later, when the desert grew blood hot, Seth rested in the shadow by a small pool of water. Here he filled his stomach with bread and cheese. He was so tired that he nearly forgot to give the donkeys their fodder. After a short rest he was on his way again.

By late afternoon the sun had moved
far behind the rocking cart. Seth was
tired. As the cart swayed he fell asleep.
He dreamt he was astride a huge beast.
Then as the beast leapt into the air Seth
tumbled from its back. He woke with his
heart beating like running hooves and
found himself sitting in soft sand. He
had rolled right off the donkey-cart.

Although it was still hot Seth shivered. Before him, shadows were being caught in endless curves of sand. He looked around him and knew he was lost. Seth felt scared and lonely.

Then, at that moment, he heard a
strange sound. Twisting around, he saw
a giant oryx. The oryx looked at Seth.
Her horns formed a giant V and the first
star shone dimly between those horns.
'Could she be the animal of my dream?'
thought Seth.

The oryx was so close that Seth could touch her flanks and see her quivering. She was in some difficulty. One of her legs was pierced by a barbed-wire thorn. Slowly, Seth moved up to the animal, making a low singing noise in his throat. With care he took out the thorn.

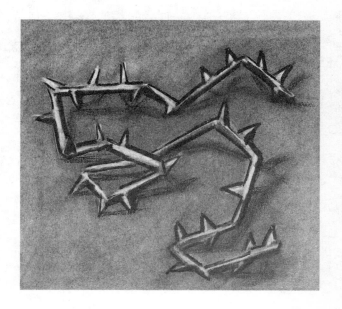

The oryx turned and Seth knew he was
to follow her. Eagerly he took up the
donkeys' reins. Together they sped across
the desert past dark yellow rocks that
looked like bits of the moon. The oryx
dipped her head and ran with the wind
of twilight. The donkeys seemed to gal-
lop at great speed. The cart rocked. As
they rushed along Seth began to make
a song about the oryx to the tune of the
cicada song.

   On this Christmas night, the sky was a
hosanna blue. As the earth gave off its
heat, the cicadas sang good-night in a
nearby tree. The last Seth saw of his oryx
was on a hill where a large rusted
water-tank stood. She lifted her beautiful
brown-black head, looked at him and
vanished.

And the evening star hung where she had stood.

Seth was wide awake. He saw that he was on the edge of a mining village. A few people were moving about. He coaxed the donkeys up the hill. Next to the water-tank was a small corrugated-iron shack, just as his grandfather had described. Seth knew he had arrived.

He took his mother's gift down from
the cart and approached the shack. He
opened the door.

There in the light of a paraffin lamp sat his mother and his father.

Between them lay their baby. His father laughed with surprise.

'It's our Seth!'

His mother held him tight against her warm body. 'You found us,' she said. 'Right in your father's shack. Come and see your new sister.'

Seth was in a great hurry to give his mother the gift he had brought so far. He tore the old newspaper off it. His fingers played across a driftwood Madonna, light as laughter. And he gave it to her.

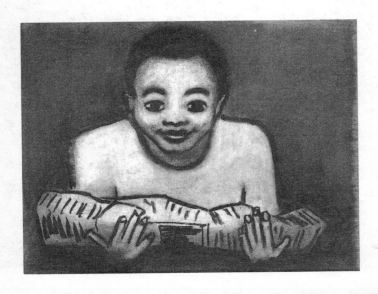

Then Seth looked at his sister. His eyes grew large with a sudden thought. He scrambled out to the cart and came back as suddenly.

'These things are for you.'

Seth put before his sister the fruit of the Nara plant and the stars in the copper rock. And he sang her his oryx song, making up the last line as he sang:

An oryx helped me find the way
When I freed her from the thorn.
Now her bright star lights the Namib sky
For my sister who is born.

Glossary

mealie   Derived from the Afrikaans word meaning 'mielie', meaning corn on the cob. Ground mealie in this instance.

oupa   Afrikaans for grandfather.
Used here as a form of address: 'old man'.

Nara plant   An edible desert plant.

veldkos   Cricketlike insects, which make a loud chirping sound.

oryx   A large antelope.

hosanna   Hosanna is a cry of praise, but is used here poetically to describe the blue of the sky.